FOREST OF FEARS

FOREST OF FEARS

Kereen Getten

Illustrated by Jemma Skidmore

Collins

Contents

Chapter 1

"Joseph!" It was Joseph's worst nightmare. Keenan was calling him over. He hesitated – nothing good ever came from talking to Keenan. From the first day Joseph had started school, Keenan had made it his mission to be mean to him. It didn't matter how hard Joseph tried to avoid them, or how much he hid in the shadows. Keenan and his friends always found him.

"I've got something to tell you; it's really important," Keenan shouted.

Maybe this time will be different, Joseph thought. *Maybe he won't be mean to me today.* Reluctantly, Joseph crossed the park towards the swings where Keenan and two of his friends were waiting.

They started laughing as he approached, and that's when Joseph knew he'd made a big mistake, but it was too late now.

"I wanted to ask you about your shoes." Keenan snickered and elbowed his friends. "Who got you those?"

Joseph stared at his feet. "My nan."

Keenan roared with laughter. He turned to his friends. "I told you. His nan chooses all his clothes and she's like, a hundred years old."

"She's 73 in two months," Joseph corrected him.

But they were already walking away, leaving Joseph standing by himself in the empty park. Joseph looked down at his black shoes. They were the only ones he liked that his nan could afford. When they went to the shop, she'd said, "You can only have the ones on sale. There's nothing wrong with them, they do the job perfectly." When her back was turned, though, he'd looked longingly at the more expensive shoes on the other shelves. The ones he knew everyone at school would be wearing.

Joseph dragged his feet the last five minutes home, allowing his old beige coat to trail over his shoes. He didn't want anyone else to see what they looked like.

It wasn't his nan's fault. She only had her pension to cover clothes and food.

As he entered the block of flats, his nan waved at him from the second floor. She was wearing a colourful headscarf covering her curly salt-and-pepper hair.

"Welcome home!" she called down to him. "Dinner is almost ready." Joseph sighed. Nan's voice was seriously loud. Sometimes he could hear her talking to the neighbours before he even reached their block of flats.

It wasn't that he didn't like his nan: he loved her. He loved her Caribbean accent, and the Jamaican food she cooked.

He loved her loud laughter that filled their flat, and the way she hummed a tune but never knew the words.

He loved the way she made him feel warm and safe. Sometimes he loved her so much, he woke up sweating and ran to her room to check she was still there.

He climbed the stairs and met her on the landing. He just wished the kids at school could see her the way he did. Like bright sunlight after a rainy morning. She was the person he loved most in the whole world. She was his best friend.

She opened the door and let him in. "How was school, my precious?" she asked.

"It was OK," said Joseph, vaguely. He dropped his bag on the floor and peeled his shoes off. He didn't mention Keenan, because it would only worry her.

Nan ruffled his hair fondly. "One day you'll be too old for school, and you'll wish you enjoyed it more." Joseph screwed his nose up. That didn't sound like him at all.

"Why don't you change out of your uniform? I'll call you when food's on the table," Nan added.

Joseph opened the first door on the left and entered his bedroom. He collapsed on his bed, staring at the ceiling above him, trying to forget the run-in with Keenan and his friends. Joseph linked his hands together and closed his eyes, ready to enter his imaginary world. The world he had created for himself.

In his world, he was everything he couldn't be in real life. In his world, he was the grandson of a chief living in the Jamaican mountains. Their tribe was cut off from the world by a menacing forest. No one made fun of him there – they liked him. In his world, everything was exactly how he wanted it to be. Well, almost everything …

Joseph's neighbourhood

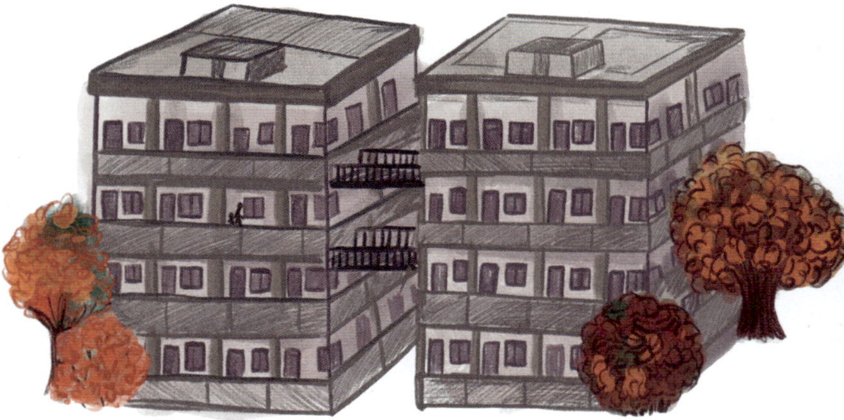

barber shop
grocery shop

school

Chapter 2

Deep in his imaginary world, Joseph chases his friends Ruben and Caleb around the village with cow poo he's collected in a wooden bowl. "Get away from me!" Caleb yells, darting between the wooden houses. Ruben giggles wildly, splitting away from Caleb. Joseph chases them around the edge of the forest, along the thin white cord that circles the village. The cord reminds them not to go beyond the line, into the forest of fears.

"Roar!" Joseph shouts, making a menacing face, and waving the cow poo at them. Suddenly, the forest roars back at them, stopping them in their tracks. *Monsters*, thinks Joseph. He turns to face the forest, as the baying of monsters fills the air.

Joseph's heart beats fast. He lives with the Maroon tribe on the outskirts of Hopeland Forest, high in the Jamaican mountains. There is only one way to their village – through the forest, guarded by monsters who prey on your fears.

Joseph has always known about the scary forest. His grandfather, the tribe leader, told him the story as soon as he was old enough to understand. He said it was their job, as leaders of the tribe, to brave the forest.

"You are getting older now, Joseph," his grandfather had said. "Your trial to face the forest is here. If you are to lead this village when I'm gone, then you must show your bravery by entering the forest alone. Everyone in our family faced the forest on their eleventh birthday. Now, it's your turn."

"I don't know if I can go in there," Joseph whispers to his friends. "I'm afraid." Ruben lays a hand on his shoulder. The forest roars louder, as though it can feel his fears.

"Joseph, dinner is ready." Nan's voice interrupted Joseph's daydreaming about the forest. He opened one eye, reluctant to come out of the world he'd created for himself. The world he knew so well. If it was up to him, he would stay in his make-believe creation forever. Even if it meant facing the forest. Grudgingly, he climbed off the bed and went over to the door.

He turned the handle and looked over his shoulder towards the bed, as though expecting to see a monster. But instead, it was just his bed. The black covers were crumpled and untidy from where he'd been lying.

"Set the table, Joseph," said Nan, as he entered the kitchen. "While I put the food out."

Joseph pulled out two beige tablemats with matching coasters. He lay them on the small table pushed against the wall. Then he pulled a chair out and sat down. Nan laid a plate of curry chicken and boiled rice with vegetables in front of him. She sat across from him, watching him closely.

"You look like the world is on your shoulders," she said gently. Joseph sat staring at his plate, and yearned to tell her about Keenan making fun of his shoes. But the last time he confided in Nan, she'd marched into school, in her headscarf and slippers, demanding to speak to the head teacher. News spread around school that his nan had come to his rescue, and everyone made fun of him. The bullying was worse than before.

"You know, your grandfather was a deep thinker like you," she said, cutting into the chicken with her knife and fork. Nan was always telling stories about her family, or Jamaica. No day went by without a story.

"Daydreamer, I'd call him. Always daydreaming." She took a bite of the piping hot chicken and stared into the distance. "I would say, 'What are you dreaming about now?' And he would reply, 'If I tell you, it won't come true, will it?'" She chuckled, shaking her head.

"Tell me," Nan went on, "what are you dreaming about in that head of yours?" Joseph thought about revealing his make-believe world that made him happy. The world where he was the grandson of a chief. Where no one bullied him, and everyone was his friend.

"Nothing," he mumbled, stuffing a forkful of food in his mouth. He didn't look at Nan, because if he did, he would see her disappointment, and he didn't want to disappoint her. For now, he would keep it to himself. He wasn't ready to share his world with anyone. Not even her.

The forest of fears

Hopeland forest
fruit trees

Chapter 3

Back in the village, Ruben throws a makeshift ball made out of old shirts. It zips through the air, above Joseph's head. He jumps to catch it, but it slips through his fingers and lands at the edge of the forest. Joseph runs over to the line that splits the village from the trees.

The wind in the trees picks up, as though his very presence makes it angry.

He uses his foot to pull the ball back over the line and picks it up with his hands. Joseph rolls the ball between his fingers, staring into the trees, his heart beating fast.

Ruben approaches him. “You don’t have to go in,” he says. “It’s pretty scary in there. I couldn’t do it.”

Joseph bites his lip, shaking his head. “I’m going in,” he says. “I’m not ready yet, that’s all.”

Ruben raises his hands in the air, walking backwards. “While we wait, throw the ball to me. If I catch it, you must try and take it from me.” Joseph attempts to block out the menacing forest, throwing the ball high in the air.

Ruben jumps to catch it. He seizes the ball, then trips and falls into a puddle of mud. “Oh no!” he cries in dismay.

Joseph shouts with laughter. “You should go into the forest yourself!” he says. “The monsters will be terrified of you, looking like that!”

"Joseph, you're going to be late for school," Nan called from the hallway. Joseph opened his eyes with a sigh. Brilliant. Another day of school! He would much rather stay home and dream about the forest and how to find the courage to go inside.

He decided to walk the long way to school. He went through the estate, towards Mr Holland's grocery shop, and Bank's the barber's, who always cut his hair too short. He walked this way because he knew Keenan and his friends took a different way.

“Good morning, Joseph.” Mr Adam, one of the teachers, gave him a nod as he entered the gates. “How are you today?” Joseph never knew how to reply to that. He was at school, so he wasn’t OK. But if he told Mr Adam that, he’d arrange a meeting with his nan, and everyone knew what happened last time a teacher did that.

“How about you do a little errand for me?” Mr Adam suggested. Joseph’s eyes lit up. He’d do anything not to be in the playground when Keenan and his friends arrived.

“I left my books in the staffroom,” said Mr Adam. “Knock on the door and ask someone to hand them to you, then take them to the 7A classroom.”

Joseph ran into the school building, heading towards the staffroom. He knocked on the door and Ms Kelly peered out. "What can I do for you, Joseph?" she asked. She always seemed annoyed about something, and she had thick eyebrows that frowned all the time.

"Mr Adam left his books and asked me to collect them," Joseph said meekly.

She looked over her shoulder and shouted, "Anyone seen Mr Adam's books?"

Ben, the receptionist, took them to the door and in turn Ms Kelly handed them to Joseph. "No hanging about in the halls," she said, shutting the door.

Joseph cradled the books in his arms and headed to Mr Adam's class. As he turned the corner, he spotted Keenan waiting outside the classroom. His heart sank. The last thing he wanted to do was deal with Keenan. Joseph thought about turning back, but he didn't want to let Mr Adam down, and Keenan had already spotted him.

"What you got there?" Keenan called out.

Joseph hesitated before approaching. "Mr Adam's books," he said.

Keenan looked at the books. "I'll take them," he said.

Joseph bit the edge of his lip. "I think I should do it," he replied.

Keenan reached for the books. "Give them, will you, he's my teacher."

Joseph wasn't persuaded by this, but Keenan seized the books and slipped them in his backpack.

Joseph eyed him suspiciously. "You will give them to him, won't you?"

Keenan widened his eyes. "Of course I will, promise."

Something told Joseph to be wary of Keenan's promises, but he didn't want to cause a fuss, so reluctantly, he walked away.

Joseph's school

7B
8A
8B
library
hall

Chapter 4

Mr Adam entered Joseph's classroom. "Joseph, can I have a word?"

Joseph's heart dropped. This didn't sound good. He followed Mr Adam into the hall.

"Do you have something for me, Joseph?"

Joseph looked at him blankly. "Sir?"

"The books, Joseph," Mr Adam replied sternly. "I know you collected them; Ms Kelly told me she gave them to you."

Joseph felt his body get hot. "I gave them to Keenan," he stammered.

"That wasn't what I asked you to do. I told you to take them to my classroom." Mr Adam shook his head in dismay. "I asked the class if anyone had seen them, and no one spoke up."

Joseph hated being in trouble. Especially when he had tried to do the right thing. "I was going to, but Keenan promised me he would do it," Joseph explained.

"Well, let's go and ask him together," Mr Adam said. Joseph followed nervously up the stairs to the classroom, hoping Keenan would do the right thing. Maybe he forgot the books were in his bag. Mr Adam opened the classroom door and called Keenan outside.

"Yes, sir?" Keenan asked innocently.

"Joseph says he gave you the books," Mr Adam stated. "Is that true?"

Keenan shook his head, "No, sir, but we found your books in the boys' toilets." He pointed to the books on his desk. Mr Adam turned to Joseph with a raised eyebrow.

"Honestly, sir, I don't know how they got there," Joseph whispered.

Mr Adam frowned. "You can go back to your class now."

Joseph turned on his heels and ran down the stairs. He should have known Keenan would stitch him up. Now Mr Adam thought he was a liar, when he was only trying to do the right thing.

"Joseph, is that you?" Nan called from the kitchen.

Joseph walked into the room where his nan was watering her plants. "Yes, it's me," he replied solemnly.

She frowned. "What's the matter with you?"

Joseph could feel the tears fill his eyes. "I don't want to go back to school," he muttered.

His nan wiped her hands on her skirt and walked towards him. She wrapped him in a big hug. "There, there," she soothed. "What happened? You can tell me anything."

She pulled out a chair at the table and sat him down. Then she seized another chair and pulled it close to his. "You know, I've been afraid of many things in my life," Nan said softly.

"But the biggest thing I was afraid of was a story in my village about a ghost that lived in the outside toilet."

Joseph swallowed. "A ghost?"

Nan nodded, placing both her hands on her knees. "I was so afraid that I couldn't go to the toilet alone. My mother had to check it was clear, then wait for me all hours of the day and night. Then, one night, I begged her to go with me, and you know what she said?" Joseph shook his head. "She said, 'Mabel, it's time you went by yourself.' I told her I couldn't do it – I was frightened. She told me she had never seen the ghost, not once. She said if there really was a ghost, and it had bad intentions, it would have done something already. She told me, 'Face the fear, and see what happens.'"

Joseph sat up in his chair. "And what happened?"

Nan laughed. "Well, it turned out my mother was right. The only thing out there was the wind in the trees, and a dog howling into the night. I still ran back to the house, just in case, but I went by myself the next night, and the next, until it wasn't scary anymore."

Joseph pondered this for some time. "I don't think I'm as brave as you," he concluded.

Nan took his face in her hands. "Try it," she said warmly. "Try it and keep trying it until, one day, you forget you're even trying."

Back in his room, Joseph closed the door, still thinking about the story Nan had told him. He threw his bag on the floor and lay on his bed staring at the ceiling. "*Keep trying until you forget you're even trying.*" Nan's words echoed in his ears as he took a deep breath and closed his eyes.

Keenan's Diary

The baby woke me up really early. Now I can't get back to sleep.

Stepdad Jake told me it was time to get up. I tried telling him I didn't get any sleep but he said: 'Try being a grownup, with responsibilities.' But I'm not a grown-up, I'm a kid!

He made me drink milk with my cereal. Mum didn't make me drink milk before he came along. As long as I had breakfast, she was happy. We were both happy.

Met up with my friends and we walked to school together, but we took the long way because we hate school.

Saw Amran with the football I wanted for Christmas, but Jake said I didn't deserve it because I had a bad report card. Jake ruins everything. So I took Amran's. Amran said he'd tell his big brother, so I gave it back. It was a rubbish colour anyway.

In class, Hamza kept pulling faces and made me laugh so hard that Mr Adam told me off. That really made me mad because why is he always picking on me and no-one else?

After school I hung out with Paulton and James. We saw Joseph and messed with him a little. He thinks he's better than us because the teachers love him. So I made fun of his shoes. They looked cheap. At least Mum buys me nice shoes.

Chapter 5

It's evening in the village. The moon is full in the sky, casting a spotlight over the houses. Joseph stands alone at the edge of the forest. He's staring into the woods, willing himself to go in. Maybe if he runs fast, he'll be too quick for the monsters. He came second last year at the school sports day.

I think I can do it, he tells himself.

Ruben approaches. "What are you doing?"

"I think I'm ready," Joseph says breathlessly.

Ruben turns on his heels. "Joseph is going into the forest!" he screams. Before Joseph has time to change his mind, the entire village has gathered around him.

His grandparents push their way through the crowd. "So, you're ready," his grandfather says solemnly. He sees the fear in Joseph's eyes and lays an arm around him, to soothe him. "I know you're afraid. I was too, when I first entered the forest. By facing your fears, Joseph, you are showing you are a leader. You will be an example to the village. They will trust you to protect them from the forest."

His grandmother pulls Joseph in close to her. "Your mind is your strongest power: use it," she whispers. "All you have to do is bring us back as many fruits as your bag can carry. The mango tree, apple tree and guava tree are all in the middle of the forest. You can't miss them." She slips a pouch over Joseph's shoulder. "The fruits mean you passed the test, but they also mean we get something delicious to eat!" she says, with a twinkle in her eyes.

Joseph takes a deep breath and closes his eyes. *I can do this,* he tells himself. He counts in his head.

One

Two

Three

His foot hovers over the white line between the village and the forest.

He inhales sharply and steps over the line. A whisper of icy air engulfs him. Joseph opens his eyes slowly. The ground beneath him feels and looks the same. It is the same ground where he and his friends always sat, legs crossed, drawing pictures in the dirt with sticks. He looks over his shoulder. His grandparents give him a nod of approval. He breathes out nervously and continues forward.

Joseph walks deeper into the forest, until he is out of sight of the village. Suddenly, the trees roar around him like guard dogs protecting their home. A strong wind circles him like a tornado. It whistles loudly in his ears, forcing him to cover them with his hands. Every step becomes harder as he fights against the wind. He closes his eyes, hoping the monsters around him will disappear. But they only get louder.

"Open your eyes, Joseph," a gentle voice whispers in his ears. The voice sounds like Nan's.

Joseph shakes his head adamantly, frozen to the spot. He's afraid that if he moves, the monsters will carry him away.

"*Open your eyes, Joseph.*"

Joseph breathes deeply. He has to open his eyes. He can't stay here forever.

"*I'm not afraid.*" He repeats it until his whispers turn to shouts and his shouts turn to screams. Suddenly, the wind stops, and the forest becomes quiet.

Joseph peers through his lashes, looking around. There are no monsters, and no Nan, only the gentle swaying of the trees.

When Joseph walks out of the forest with his pouch filled with mangoes, apples and guavas, the villagers erupt into cheers. His grandparents welcome him with open arms. "You did it, grandson," his grandfather beams. "You faced your fears. I'm so proud of you."

"You have nothing to fear anymore," his grandfather adds. "Now the village trusts you to protect everyone, and the forest knows you are no longer afraid."

The villagers swarm towards him and lift him above their heads, victoriously carrying him back to the village.

Joseph jumped out of his dream, exhilarated. He rushed down the hall into their tiny living room, where Nan was watching her television show. He threw his arms around her tightly.

"Whoa, what's this?" she cried.

Joseph rested his head on her shoulder. "Thank you for helping me to be brave," he whispered.

She kissed his head. "Not me," she said softly. "I didn't do anything; it was all you, my little prince. It was all you."

Nan's scrapbook

Chapter 6

Joseph had a brilliant day at school. First: he got the highest Maths results in the class. Second: there was a new girl sitting next to him who talked to him a lot. Her name was Eleanor.

Joseph's happiness didn't last long, however. At break, Keenan and his friends hovered in the hallway, blocking his path.

Keenan nudged his friends. "Hey, it's Joseph. He lives with his old nan!"

"I do," said Joseph. "But why do you care so much?" Something had changed. Fear of Keenan would no longer plague him.

Mr Adam appeared around the corner. "You're not getting in trouble again, are you, Keenan?" he warned. "You know what happens if you are. We call your father in for a meeting." Keenan's face turned ashen and Joseph saw how scared he was. *Maybe he has a strict father*, Joseph thought.

"Joseph?" Mr Adam glanced at him seriously. "Is everything OK here?"

Joseph pondered his reply. Keenan looked so afraid. He didn't want him to get in trouble. "Yes, fine. We were talking about our families," Joseph explained to Mr Adam. Keenan gave him a grateful smile.

"Well, it's home time, so vacate the hall, please," said Mr Adam.

As Mr Adam walked away, Keenan offered Joseph his hand. "Thanks, mate," he said. The boys separated and Joseph headed towards the doors.

"Joseph. Wait!" Paulton from Keenan's group caught up with him. "Can I walk with you?"

“What about your friends?” Joseph asked.

Paulton shrugged. “I don’t think I want to be friends with them anymore.”

They opened the school doors and walked outside.

“My family is different too,” Paulton said quietly. “I live with my sister and her baby. I don’t tell people. I don’t want them to make fun of me,” he admitted sheepishly.

Joseph thought about this. "Living with your sister sounds cool," he said.

Paulton scoffed. "Oh no, she's strict. When Mum was too ill to look after me, she didn't want me to think I could just do whatever. So, she has loads more rules than Mum."

"Really?" Joseph said curiously. "Like what?"

Paulton ticked off the list on his fingers. "Homework as soon as I get in. Chores or I don't go to football practice."

"She sounds like my nan," Joseph replied. An idea suddenly came to him. "You should come for my birthday tea and meet my nan."

Paulton's eyes lit up. "She would have to talk to my sister," he said.

Joseph opened his bag and took out his phone. "Take my number. I bet your sister says yes. Everyone loves my nan."

"They're here!" Joseph shouted, opening the front door before anyone had time to ring the bell. Paulton and Eleanor stood outside, with Paulton's sister and Eleanor's father.

They handed him birthday cards and he ripped them open with delight.

While his nan talked to the adults, Joseph and his new friends set the table for Nan's Jamaican soup.

"I'm sorry about Keenan," Paulton said. "I only hung out with him because I was afraid of him."

"I understand," Joseph replied. "I know what it's like to be afraid."

They tucked into Nan's soup and compared notes on their hobbies and what they could do together.

"Do you have a bike?" Paulton asked, with his mouth full. "They have bike ramps in the park."

"I've got one," Eleanor said. "I haven't used it in ages, though. It's in the garage."

"I had a bike when I was eight," Joseph said. "We gave it to Chris upstairs. I'll ask if I can borrow it."

Paulton chuckled into his hand. "You'd look brilliant riding a kid's bike!" They fell into loud chatter, comparing funny scenarios of Joseph on a tiny bike.

At the end of the evening, Joseph walked them out.

"Park on Saturday?" Eleanor queried. They all agreed.

"Then maybe we can do something after?" Paulton said. Joseph watched them leave, before closing the door.

"How was that?" Nan asked, peering around the living room door.

Joseph sighed with contentment. “The best.”

When he entered his bedroom, he didn’t lie on the bed to enter his imaginary world like he usually did. Instead, he went over to his desk by the window and started making a list of things to do with his new friends.

Family photos

Joseph and his nan

Paulton,
his sister and
her baby

Eleanor and her family

Keenan and his family

About the author

Kereen Getten

What kind of books do you love to write?

I love writing mystery and adventure books. I like to take the character on an exciting experience that is filled with wonder. Where they learn more about themselves and become more confident.

Where did you get the idea for this book?

I'm never quite sure where my ideas come from. They just appear! For this story the forest came to me at once, and the idea that the character was escaping into an imaginary world.

Why did you want to write this book?

Joseph's story was an exciting one to explore. I liked the idea of his real world and imaginary world living side by side.

Are any of the characters based on real people?

There are some elements of myself in this story, but mostly, all the characters are fictional.

Which illustration do you like best?

I love the illustrations with the forest as they bring Joseph's imagination to life.

Does anything in this book relate to your own experiences?

Yes, my family moved houses often. I was always the new kid at school, often in towns where my sister and I were the only black children. Like Joseph, I would use my imagination to escape my reality .

What do you hope readers will get from this book?

I hope they will have empathy for the quieter child in their school and for the child who is new or struggling to fit in. For the reader who can relate to Joseph because of their own experience, I hope this story gives you hope that it gets better. I hope you feel seen, and I hope you have a Paulton or a Nan you can confide in.

What advice would you give to someone who wants to be a writer?

Read as much as you can and write as often as you can. Reading will teach you how to put a story together. As with any skill, if you practise writing consistently, you will get better and better. But more importantly, don't be hard on yourself. Published authors go through many, many edits before you see the finished product. We all start at the same place, with just an idea.

About the illustrator

What made you want to be an illustrator?

Jemma Skidmore

When I was younger, I read so many amazing books and fell in love with the pictures. I always struggled with reading because I'm dyslexic, so the pictures were really important to me. I could read a lot more detail in the illustrations than I could in the text. However, I didn't realise I could do it as a job until I was 30!

How did you get into illustration?

I spent a lot of time building film sets. I worked really long days, then had gaps of time off. In those breaks, I started painting. My first move into illustration was painting picture books for film sets – then I moved on to actual picture books.

Do you identify with anyone in the story?

I think Joseph. When I was a kid, I spent a lot of time escaping into my imagination. He seems like he will grow up to have a creative job – working on film sets or drawing things from his imagination.

What materials do you use to illustrate?

I normally paint traditionally – there's nothing better than paint and paper. But I start all of my images on an iPad.

Which scene in the book did you enjoy illustrating the most?

I loved painting the family photos for Joseph's friends. The best bits are when I get to illustrate things that aren't in the text. It's like when you read a book and fill in the gaps with your imagination.

Which scene did you find the trickiest ?

I found the maps pretty tricky! They're in a different style from my usual work. But it was great to try something new!

Did you prefer illustrating the real world or Joseph's fantasy world?

It's hard to pick! I tried to tell the story with the different environments. When Joseph is feeling low, his surroundings are dark and scary. But when he's around his nan, everything is full of plants, joy, and happiness. As Joseph's confidence grows, the colours get a bit brighter. I think the way we feel affects how we see the world around us, and I tried to show that through my drawings.

Book chat

When you saw the cover, what did you think this book was about? Were you right?

Do any of the characters change from the start of the book to the end?

Are there any similarities between Joseph's real and fantasy worlds?

How does Joseph's fantasy world help him?

Who would you recommend this book to and why?

If you could talk to any character from this book, who would you pick and what would you say?

Which part of the book did you like best?

If you had to think of a different title for the book, what would you choose?

Do you like the ending of this book? Why or why not?

Book challenge:

Draw a map of your own fantasy world.

Collins
BIG CAT

Published by Collins An imprint of HarperCollins*Publishers*

The News Building
1 London Bridge Street
London
SE1 9GF
UK

Macken House
39/40 Mayor Street Upper
Dublin 1
D01 C9W8
Ireland

10 9 8 7 6 5 4 3 2 1

ISBN 978-0-00-874638-4

British Library Cataloguing-in-Publication Data
A catalogue record for this publication is available from the British Library.

Download the teaching notes and word cards to accompany this book at: http://littlewandle.org.uk/signupfluency/

Author: Kereen Getten
Illustrator: Jemma Skidmore (Bright Agency)
Publisher: Laura White
Product manager and commissioning editor: Caroline Green
Series editor: Charlotte Raby
Phonics consultant: Catherine Baker
Project manager: Emily Hooton
Copyeditor: Sally Byford
Proofreader: Catherine Dakin
Cover designer: Sarah Finan
Typesetter: 2Hoots Publishing Services Ltd
Production controller: Katharine Willard

Printed in the UK

FSC www.fsc.org
MIX
Paper | Supporting responsible forestry
FSC™ C007454

This book contains FSC™ certified paper and other controlled sources to ensure responsible forest management.

For more information visit: www.harpercollins.co.uk/green

Made with responsibly sourced paper and vegetable ink

Scan to see how we are reducing our environmental impact.